Dedication

To my friend Lori, thank you for encouraging me to adopt a pet.
To My Daughter Raquel. I am grateful that you inspired me to write
this story and for your love of animals.
Danielle, you captured my vision of the characters and made the
illustrations fun and exciting. This is just the beginning. Your
talent will open doors for you.
Autumn, thank you for being my first reader!

To my readers don't forget to Keep the Faith!

- Sonia Suber

Spartacus Gets Adopted Sonia Suber
Available Formats: eBook Paperback distribution

Spartacus
Gets
Adopted

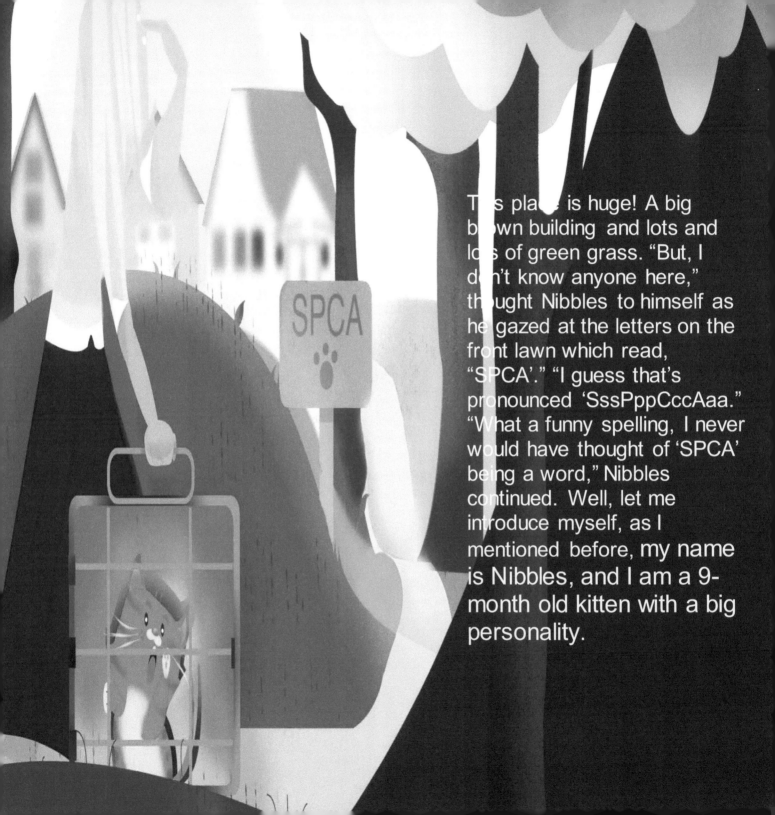

This place is huge! A big brown building and lots and lots of green grass. "But, I don't know anyone here," thought Nibbles to himself as he gazed at the letters on the front lawn which read, "SPCA'." "I guess that's pronounced 'SssPppCccAaa." "What a funny spelling, I never would have thought of 'SPCA' being a word," Nibbles continued. Well, let me introduce myself, as I mentioned before, my name is Nibbles, and I am a 9-month old kitten with a big personality.

"Why is my owner dropping me off here?" I wondered.
They are talking about me and I hear them call my name,
"Nibbles." "Yes that's me," I mumbled in my head! What! I just
heard her say that I didn't play well with the other cats.
Hey! That's not true." She said I liked to nibble on fingers. Well that
means I like you and plus I am teething, that's all, just teething.
You know everybody teeth's right and what's wrong with that?
She said I fight with the other cats. "Well they wrestled me first."
Didn't you see them tackle me first and that's not fighting, I call that
playing. That's what we kittens do, we play and we wrestle!

Oh no! Wait, why is she leaving me? "Hey wait!! Don't go. Don't
leave me here," Nibbles kept quiet, but he was really thinking,
"Where are they taking me?" "It smells really strange here. Why
are they putting me in this big metal cage? I don't belong here!! I
have a home. Who are these other cats? I don't know them?" With
my biggest voice, I started to cry, "MEOW, MEOW, MEOW."

I must have caused such a fuss because a lady in a white coat
looked down at me and said, "Nibbles, welcome to SPCA."
With the prettiest smile on her face she said, "You are in
quarantine for a week until we make sure you are healthy to go out
and be with the other cats.

"Don't be afraid," she said. "We are going to take good care of you here and hopefully you will be adopted soon."

I soon found myself feeling at ease because this lady seemed to be really nice.

Then I thought, "ADOPTED?!"
"Why am I being given away? What does SPCA mean anyway.
I want to go home," I muttered sorrowfully to myself. There was
a blanket and bowl of water in my cage. I curled up on the
blanket in a ball hoping my owner would soon come back and
get me.

I could see across from my cage other cages with cats. Some of the other cats were probably about the same age as I was; and other cats were older and bigger than me.

I thought to myself, "These cats are in QUARANTINE too. Just like me with hopes of being adopted."
"With so many kittens and cats, how long will it take for me to get adopted? Will someone pick me? Who would want a kitten like me with a BIG Personality," sadly, I wondered to myself. "I am scared, but I know I have to be brave," I said.

Later, I soon found out there was more than one person who wore white coats. They came towards me and talk to me. They refilled my food and water bowl. Although there were people and other cats around, I felt lonely. A blue light lit the room to make the dark not seem so scary; but I was still scared. I missed my human family and cat friends.

chapter 2

The next morning the nice lady in the white coat came back and wished me a good morning. "Hello Nibbles, my name is Lori," she said. "Today you need to get your next round of kitty shots." "What are kitty shots?" Quickly, she opened the cage and wrapped me in a blanket and took me to this big room. The room was white and gray with bright lights. She sat me on a cold table, unwrapped the blanket and stuck me with this sharp needle in my hip. I quickly jumped and meowed. She stuck me again.

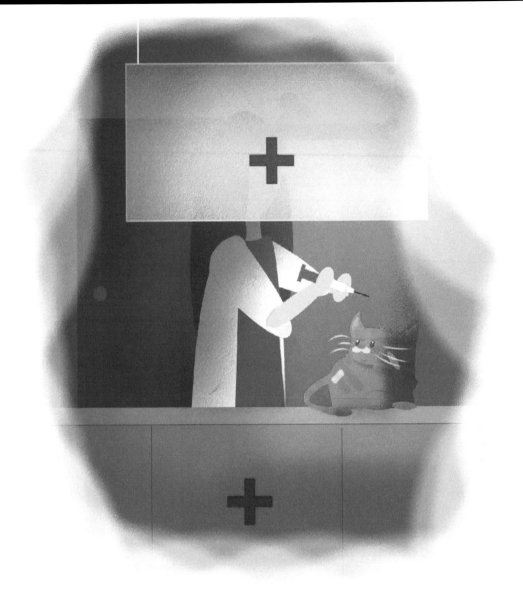

"Ouch! Stop that! It hurts," I wanted to tell her.
But I kept quiet as she began to wrap the blanket around me.
She picked me up and carried me back to my cage.

Those shots made my hip hurt and I felt very very woozy.
So, off I went to sleep.

Y

A

W

N

The next day I got to go to the playroom.
I walked around feeling sad and lonely.
There were other cats in the playroom.

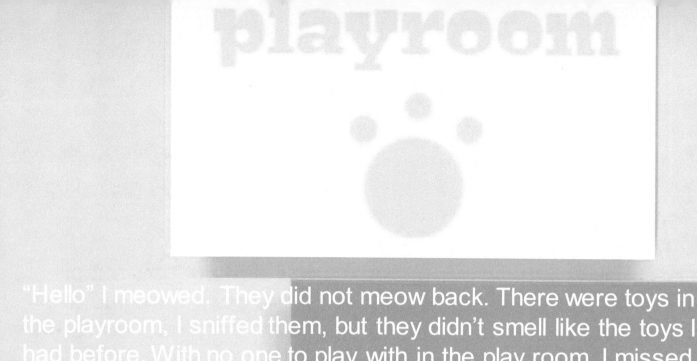

"Hello" I meowed. They did not meow back. There were toys in the playroom, I sniffed them, but they didn't smell like the toys I had before. With no one to play with in the play room, I missed my friends. I missed wrestling. I missed jumping on my friend's back and tugging at their ears. I missed all of the fun things we did together. Oh well, back into the cage I went.

"I really don't like this place," I mumbled to myself. "I want to go home." Later, Lori came to my cage while I was curled up and looking at my surrounding's.

"Hi Nibbles, your time is up," she said. "You are now out of quarantine and will be moved with all the other cats who are ready for adoption." "Ready for adoption. Me! You mean I am not going back home? I guess not," I thought sadly. "Will anyone want to adopt me? Will it be a boy or girl? Will they have other pets? Will the pets like me? If they don't will, I end up back at this place called the SssPppCccAaa?" I asked. "Oh no they are moving me. They are taking me out of my cage and moving me to another area."

Chapter 3

There was a cage with my name printed on a tan card and it said, "NIBBLES". There were lots of older cats in there. Then I thought, "I have been here for a week and I don't know what day it is." They had placed me across from this one cat. I could not see his name plate. I asked, "Excuse me. Can you tell me what day it is?" He meowed, "Friday, the 28th." "Thank you," I said."

I asked the cat who looked to be 2 years old, "How long have you been here?" "30 days," he said. "I had to spend 7 days in quarantine, you know."

"Oh no! 30 days. I don't want to be here 30 days. I want a home like I had before. I want a family of my own," I insisted. "What's your name kid?" he asked. "Nibbles." He laughed, "That's a cute name. "He chuckled again, "Don't worry Nibbles, it's your first day. You may get lucky."

"It's not so bad here. They take good care of you and you get to meet lots of visitors. People walk around and look at us in our cages. If they like what they see, off to the playroom we go. They see how we respond to our perspective new family. If they like us, we get adopted. By the way, I'm Simba." "Hi Simba. How many times have you been to the playroom?" I asked. Simba turned his head and looked up at the ceiling and said, "Three times so far. It's been slow here since it's the holiday and all. But I like it here. I know I will get adopted soon. You have to stay positive kid and keep the faith."

"What is faith Simba?" "Well, faith is when you believe in your heart something so strong even if you can't see it with your own eyes, you know it's going to happen. You feel it, faith tingles and moves all through- out your body. You got that kid." I said, "Yeah, I got it." Simba gave me one more piece of advice.

"Make sure you clean yourself up kid and be friendly. It will get you far. The new family, especially when they bring the kids, like it when we are friendly and playful. And no biting or scratching. Okay, Kid?" "I got it Simba," I said with excitement.

There was hope, I could get adopted soon. Simba was nice to me and he made me feel so much better. So, I started grooming my coat and walking around in my cage saying to myself keep the faith, get adopted. Keep the faith, get adopted. While waiting to get adopted I had that thing tingling all through me which Simba called faith. I started believing I would get adopted.

Chapter 4

It was lunchtime and all these people started to come in. I noticed Simba had cleaned his coat. Simba had long fur and it was nice and full. His fur was a mixture of black and brown. Simba had the biggest paws. I can tell he was a proud Calico cat by the way he sat tall in his cage; but he was so gentle and caring. He called my name, "Nibbles are you ready to meet the visitors." "Yes, I am Simba!" "All right then," he said. "Let's do this Nibbles" He chuckled, "Nibbles what a name Kid!"

There were many people from what I could see, but there was only one who came to my cage. She was pretty with ponytails and light brown skin like my coat. "Hello Nibbles," she said. I meowed and walked back and forth as my orange brown fur rubbed against the cage. I wanted her to touch my soft coat. She said, "Hey Kitty". I continued to walk back and forth. Simba meowed, "Just be yourself Kid; I think she likes you." Suddenly, I heard a young girl yell, "Mom I like him. I want him." She looked to be 10 years old. Her Mom said, "Which one."

"This one over here, his name is Nibbles." "I wonder why they named him Nibbles," Her Mom said. I heard the Mom call the little girl Raquel. I am guessing that's her human name. I thought that was a pretty name.

Chapter 5

Raquel's mom asked Lori to take me to the playroom. I remembered what Simba said, "be friendly! I kept repeating to myself. "Be friendly. Be friendly. "I was excited! As Lori stood with me and my visitors, she explained this was my first day out of quarantine. "I don't like the word quarantine or the place itself," I thought to myself. Lori told my guest that I was dropped off because I didn't play well with the other cats.

I was thinking again, "That's not true." She said I would fight the other cats. Not true, I was just playing with them. You know wrestling. She also told them I had a bad habit of biting. My previous family could not stop me from biting her or her kids. I said to myself, "those were love bites. You know like little nibbles. I was showing affection that's all, plus I am teething. Maybe that's why they named me Nibbles. Well that's not a name for a strong, brave and adventurous cat like me!" Back to the present, I have to stay focused, no distractions.
Raquel must get to know the true me. The cat who likes to run, play and cuddle and most of all show affection through a few love bites, you know nibbles.

Raquel's mom said to her, "You sure you can handle him? It doesn't appear he plays well with others and he likes to bite." I walked back and forth next to Raquel while rubbing my nice bright orange brown coat against her legs. I wanted to show her that I was not a naughty cat. Raquel was sitting on a bench. I had an urge to jump in her lap, so she could rub me. So, I did it. I jumped right into her lap, but I was sure to keep my claws in, so I would not scratch her. I had not been rubbed in a week and boy did I miss that feeling.

Raquel yelled, "WOW Mom he is so friendly."
I rubbed my soft whiskers against her chubby cheeks, and I remembered to PURRRR. She laughed and said, "Mom, can I have him." Out of nowhere, her Mom said, "Are you sure? He sounds like a handful." "He maybe a handful but I think we can handle him," Raquel said. I looked at Raquel's Mom and meowed, "Oh, please pick me to go home with you. I think Raquel will be so much fun to play with. Please, oh please Raquel's mom say yes." Raquel's mom finally said, "Okay we will take Nibbles." Raquel yelled, "YESS!" "Okay, I'll take Nibbles with me and you two go to the front desk to complete your Cat adoption papers," Lori said. "She said yes! She said yes," I thought in delight as I went to the back to get checked out as a newly adopted cat. I saw Simba going into the playroom. I meowed to him, "Simba, it worked. I am getting adopted!" He meowed, "Good for you kid, and guess what, I think I am a winner here too and will be the next cat out the door. So, long Kid." "See what having faith can do!" I was so excited. I was getting adopted. How will my new home be? Hopefully nice. Will I have to share my sleeping quarters with other cats? Will I have to share my food bowl? Oh, will I have any toys? Most of all will Raquel and her mom love me no matter what?

Chapter 6

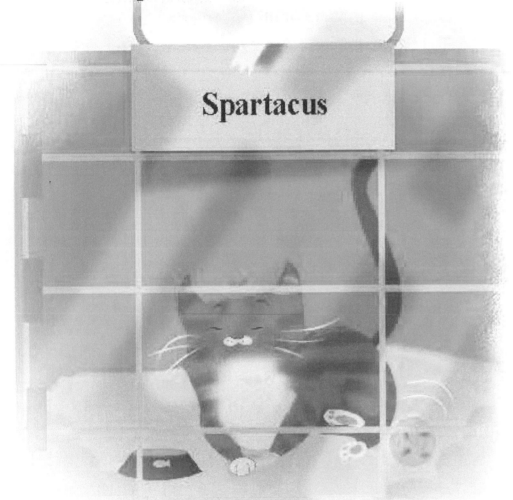

Spartacus

Finally, they brought me out to Raquel and mom. They had a blue cat carrier ready for me. The clerk said, "Well Nibbles you have a new name. "I do? What is it? What is it?" "Raquel has named you SPARTACUS. Here are your new tags with your name printed along with your family's name and phone number just in case you get lost."

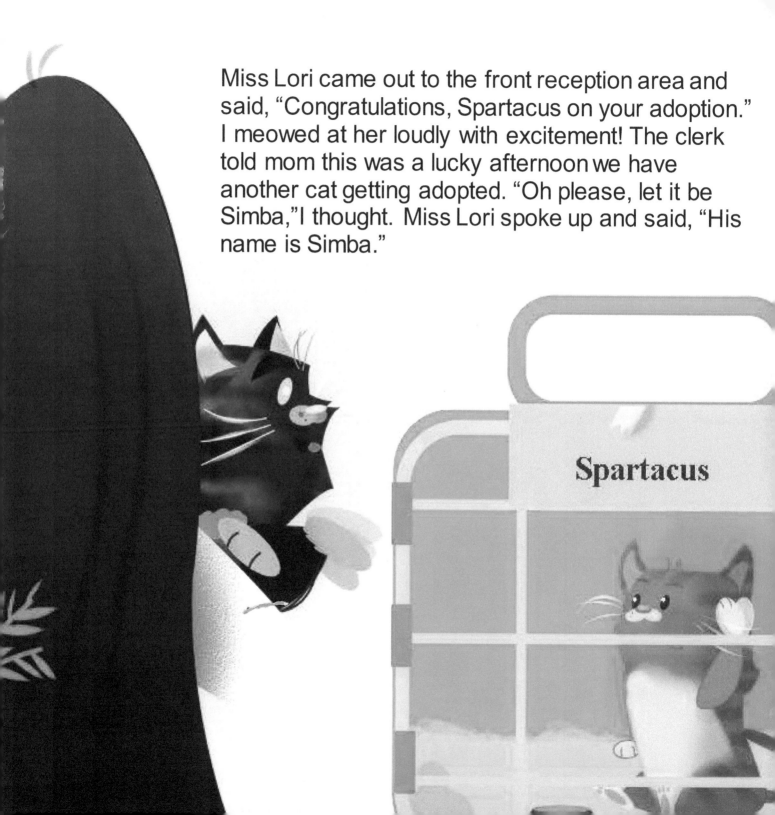

Miss Lori came out to the front reception area and said, "Congratulations, Spartacus on your adoption." I meowed at her loudly with excitement! The clerk told mom this was a lucky afternoon we have another cat getting adopted. "Oh please, let it be Simba," I thought. Miss Lori spoke up and said, "His name is Simba."

Spartacus

Today is a good day at the Society Prevention for the Cruelty to Animals, there is something special when an animal gets a new home and a second chance. That's what SssPppCccAaa stands for. The SPCA gives cat's like me a second chance. Second chances and faith, they go together!

I am adopted! I am adopted! I have a new name. Simba has a new home. Yes, today is a good day at the SPCA. They put me in the carrier. Raquel peeped in and said, "Hey Spartacus. We are going to take you to your new home. No longer will you be called Nibbles; your personality is too big for that! We are going to call you Spartacus or Sparty for short." I think I like that name. Simba would be proud of my new name.

"You will have your own bed, your own water and food bowl and all of the toys you want. And, I am going to give you so much love and kitty hugs, alright my Spartacus," she said. "Alright my Raquel, let's go home," I meowed loudly.

VOCABULARY LIST

Adventurous: Willing to take risk or try out new ideas or experiences

Affection: A gentle feeling of liking

Distractions: A thing that prevents someone from giving full attention to something

Faith: When you believe in your heart something so strong even if you can't see it with your own eyes, but you believe.

Quarantine: A place in which people or animals that have arrived from elsewhere are held.

Reception area: A large open area near the entrance of a building. Sleeping quarters: An assigned space to sleep.

SPCA: The SPCA (Society for the Prevention of Cruelty to Animals) is dedicated to preventing cruelty towards animals. In addition to protecting and providing shelter to strays and animals in danger, the SPCA deals with proper pet care and animal adoption.

As an exercise please review the book and find additional words to add to the vocabulary list.

Spartacus Gets Adopted
tells the story of a kitty named Nibbles, who gets returned
to the SPCA, in hopes of being adopted a second time.
Nibbles must learn to keep the Faith no matter how
disappointed because
inspiring things can happen!

About the author,

Sonia Suber always had a love for animals.
Her wish is for all animals to be adopted into a safe
and loving environment.

CPSIA information can be obtained
at www.ICGtesting.com
Printed in the USA
LVHW071941140820
663220LV00002B/15